OH THOSE CRAZY DOGS!

TEDDI BEAR AND COLBY LOVE SWIMMING IN THE POOL

CAL

ILLUSTRATED BY:
RACHAEL PLAQUET

BOOK FIVE

To order additional copies of this book, contact:
Xlibris
844-714-8691
www.Xlibris.com
Orders@Xlibris.com

ISBN: Softcover   978-1-6698-0358-4
       Hardcover   978-1-6698-0359-1
       EBook   978-1-6698-0357-7

Print information available on the last page

Rev. date: 12/23/2021

OH! THOSE CRAZY DOGS!

TEDDI BEAR AND COLBY LOVE SWIMMING IN THE POOL

Introduction

This is a story about 2 crazy dogs, their adventures and the mischief they get into.

They are very loving dogs, but they can't help getting into things.

Hi ! I'm Colby! I'm big and red and furry ! I love everyone but sometimes people are afraid of me because I am so big!

Hi ! I'm Teddy Bear! I'm big and white and very furry! I'm not as big as Colby, but just about. Everyone thinks I'm cute and I put shows on for them.

Our owners picked us out specially and brought us home
to love and care for us. We love them too, very much.
They give us everything we want and a warm loving home.
We will call them Mom and Pop

Sometimes we don't listen to them, especially me, Teddi Bear!

but our Mom and Pop love us anyway. Sometimes I get Colby in trouble. I can get him to do anything I want because he loves me too and can't say no. He protects me all the time.

TEDDI BEAR AND COLBY LOVE SWIMMING IN THE POOL

Teddi Bear and Colby ran to the patio door as soon as they saw mom getting out towels and changing into less clothes.

Teddi Bear started jumping up on mom and barking excitedly

"Down Teddi Bear", said mom. Mom opened the patio doors and out ran Colby and Teddi Bear racing to the pool !

Colby ran straight down the steps and into the water to swim around the pool.

Teddi Bear ran around the pool to the other side and perched at the edge, waiting for someone to throw his rubber bone that he always played with in the pool.

Mom picks up his bone and says," ready, set, go!" and throws his bone in the pool.

Teddi Bear jumps for the bone.

and lands in the water right beside the bone.

He snaps at the bone and gets it the first time.

Teddi looks for mom.

And he sees her in the pool close to him.

"Nooo! Mom is going to take my bone!" Teddi Bear races toward the steps to get out, before mom catches him.

Mom is close behind him. Mom says "I'm going to get that bone! Watch out, I'm going to get that bone!"

Teddi quickly climbs up the steps with the bone in his mouth.

Teddi Bear turns his head and looks at mom, "hah you can't catch me!" and runs along the edge of the pool.

Mom stays in the pool, swimming and waiting for Teddi Bear to drop his bone.

Teddi Bear drops the bone by one of mom's large planters

and runs back to the same place as before, assuming the same position as before.

Mom swims over to where Teddi Bear dropped the bone, picks it up and says," ready, set, go!" And throws the bone again.

Teddi Bear jumps up and goes flying over the pool !

He catches the bone in mid air, lands in the pool with a big splash!

Teddi Bear swims toward the steps as fast as he can.
Teddi Bear looks back,

He spots mom trying to catch up to him. "Nooo, she's after me again!" He speeds up and runs up the steps and out of the pool!

Teddi Bear puts the bone in the same place as before,

and runs around the pool to the exact same place as before.

Meanwhile, Colby decides to go for another swim around the pool. He goes all around the edges of the pool and then gets out, shaking all over pop!

Pop throws Colby's whirligig toward the pool and says "Colby go and get it". Mom grabs it midair and calls to Colby," come and get it!" and starts swimming toward the deep end.

Then mom starts to swim away with the whirligig and Colby jumps in and starts swimming fast toward her. Mom gets to the end of the pool and lets go of the whirligig then moves away from it because Colby is very strong and she wouldn't want him to scratch her!

Colby gets the whirligig and swims back to the steps.

Colby decides to lie down with the whirligig on the brick patio under the wisteria vine and stays in the shade.

Teddi Bear decides he doesn't want to wait until mom throws his bone for him and starts barking.

Mom, who is still in the pool, pretends to ignore him with her back turned to him.

Teddi Bear runs to where he put the bone and pokes it a couple of times

Teddi Bear looks at Mom again and barks. " It's here mom, it's here!" mom ignores him, trying not to laugh, so Teddi Bear runs around the pool, goes down the stairs and swims to the spot where his bone is. He treads water at the spot and barks at mom again." It's here mom, you can get it from here, see?"

Mom starts to swim over and Teddi Bear races out of the pool and over to his original spot and assumes his lurch position. Mom throws the bone for Teddi Bear again. Teddi Bear jumps and goes flying through the air again and catches his bone when he lands in the water.

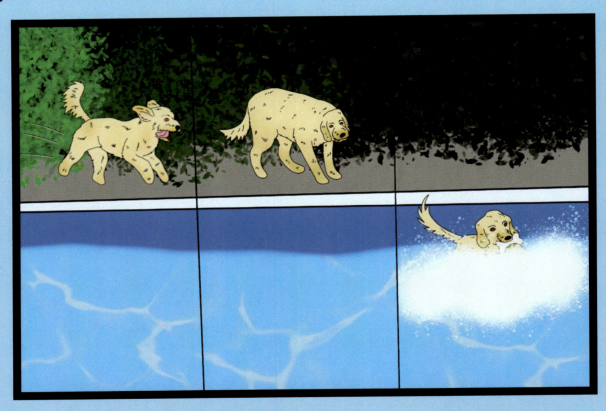

Teddi Bear races up the steps, drops his bone, and shakes water all over pop.

Then he goes over to Colby and takes his whirligig, runs away with it and drops the whirligig into the pool.

Colby gets up and goes to the side of the pool and paws the water to try to get the whirligig to come closer.

the whirligig slowly gets closer to the edge and Colby bends down and grabs the whirligig in his mouth.

He runs back to his shady spot under the vine and puts his head down on his whirligig.

Pop comes out of the house with treats in his hand.

He asked mom, who was still in the pool, if she wanted to give the treats to the dogs.

Mom took the treats and started swimming backward with the treats in her hand saying "come on Colby, come on Teddi. Come and get them!"

Colby and Teddi Bear both jump into the water and swim really fast to mom.

She gives one treat to each dog when they get to her. Mom grabs Teddi Bears bone again and is laughing as she swims away from him.

Teddi Bear swims as fast as he can to catch up to her.

When Teddi Bear finally catches up to Mom, she throws the bone toward the other end of the pool.

Teddi bear turns very fast and races to catch the bone, while he looks backward to see if mom is trying to follow him.

Mom says," I'm going to get you, I'm going to get you" as she swim's toward Teddi Bear.

Teddi Bear takes off as fast as he can and runs up the steps!

He shakes water all over pop again and lies down beside him with his bone in his mouth.

Mom exclaimed," I think Teddi Bear is finally getting tired !" Pop said, "it's about time! He has been swimming for a couple of hours!" Mom said " good I can swim the way I like now." Mom dives under the water and swims toward the end.

When she comes up above the water, Colby is standing right above her. He had been sleeping but as soon as mom dove under the water Colby got up very fast and followed her until she came above the water. He starts to bark at mom. Pop says, "he doesn't like you going under the water. Colby was very worried about you. He is your protector."

Mom gives Colby a big hug and says, "it's ok baby, mom loves to swim underwater!"

After Colby and Teddi Bear have dried off, they all go into the house and mom and pop give them their dinner.

Colby and Teddi Bear are tired now and lie down to go to sleep. Teddi Bear starts dreaming about swimming again tomorrow.

Mom and pop just shake their heads and say

OH THOSE CRAZY DOGS !!!

Thank you for reading this book and we hope you look forward to our next book about Colby and Teddi Bear and their adventures.

Books in the Oh! Those Crazy Dogs! series by author CAL

Book 1 Colby Comes Home

Book 2 Teddi Bear Comes Home

Book 3 Teddi's First Time at the Cottage

Book 4 A New Friend in the Neighborhood! Digger!

Book 5 Teddi Bear and Colby Love Swimming in the Pool

Book 6 Colby and Teddi Bear Go to the Circus

Book 7 Coming Soon!

Printed in the United States
by Baker & Taylor Publisher Services